Boo

and the Team

MIKE JAMES

Text copyright © Mike James 2012
ISBN: 9781922022141
Published by Vivid Publishing
P.O. Box 948, Fremantle
Western Australia 6959
www.vividpublishing.com.au

Chapters

1

Sheep

As the plane lifted off, Bootsie looked out the window and watched the ground beneath him get further and further away. Although he had enjoyed his time at Charlton Hall he couldn't wait to return to his real home where his heart really was. Bootsie breathed a sigh of relief when at last the plane touched down on his home soil. He wasn't a huge fan of flying in any sense and when the exit doors opened he was one of the first ones to get off the plane.

A large group of family and friends had come to the airport to welcome them home; even Bootsie had to admit it was nice to see most of his extended family again. There was a lot of hugging, talking and laughing.

"Haven't you grown?" said Bootsie's grandmother.

"Look at these guns," said one of his uncles as he began squeezing the muscles in Bootsie's arm.

"Been spending time in the gym have you?" said someone else.

It was good to be back.

One person who couldn't get over how much Bootsie had grown was Robbie. When Bootsie went down the street to see his old friend, Robbie hardly recognised him.

"Bootsie is that you?" a stunned Robbie asked.

"I think so," replied Bootsie.

"What did they feed you over there?" asked Robbie.

"Lots," replied Bootsie with a grin.

It was great for Bootsie to catch up with Robbie again. The last time they'd spent any time together was just before Bootsie left for his first year at All Kings and that had been a difficult time for both boys. Bootsie also wanted to catch up with his friend Dan, and Dan's dad.

"Look at the muscles on Bootsie," Dan's dad said as Bootsie walked into the boxing club one afternoon. "Been hitting the weights boy?"

"Yeah a bit," replied Bootsie.

"A bit, I think more than a bit. Good to see too, I'll put you in with the heavyweights if you like," Dan's dad added with a smile.

"No thanks, I'll stick with the rugby," replied Bootsie, as he looked over at some of the real heavyweight boxers hitting the various punching bags around the gym.

"Where's Dan?" Bootsie asked Dan's dad, who was busy in the ring working with another boy.

"Gone off the rails, the silly boy," he replied to Bootsie's question.

"Off the rails?" asked Bootsie, not knowing what Dan's dad had meant.

"He got mixed up with a bad crowd and for some reason went along with their stupid ideas. He ended up in a stolen car one night that had been involved in a robbery and now he's spending his days in a facility with lots of bars around him," replied Dan's dad as he told the boy he was training in the ring to take a break.

"When did all this happen?" asked Bootsie.

"Last year. He'll be out soon. He reckons he's learnt his lesson and has been training pretty hard where he is. Actually he probably doesn't get much choice. I can imagine there's some tough boys in that place just lining up to get a crack at the policeman's son. I think it's been a real wake-up call for him. Anyway we'll see when he gets out if he can put it behind him and make something of his life," he continued.

Bootsie walked away from the boxing gym stunned, he had no idea about Dan and even Robbie was unaware of what had happened to him. "I thought Dan would be the last person to end up getting into trouble like that," Bootsie said to an equally stunned Robbie.

"You're not wrong, I can't believe he would be so stupid as to mix with that crowd. I know who his dad was talking about and they're one pretty messed-up family," replied Robbie.

"Dan always was easily led though," added Bootsie, "Remember if you ever dared him to do anything he would always do it? That's why we called him 'Daredevil Dan'."

One thing that had been drilled into Bootsie from a young age was never to be a sheep, never follow the flock and *always* stand up for yourself if you think something's not right.

"If people don't like you for who *you* are then that's *their* problem," his dad had said to him once and it was something that Bootsie always remembered. Robbie was also quite headstrong and wouldn't be pushed around or act differently when other people were around. What you saw was what you got and Bootsie liked him for it. He had overcome the loss of Chris and Chris' dad (Mr Butkiss) very well, considering how hard it had initially hit him. He could have used it as an excuse for the rest of his life but he didn't. He eventually found the inner strength to move on and do something positive. Robbie had become one of the star players for the region in his age group and had played in every game at fly half.

When the two boys went down to the rugby field one day, Bootsie was amazed how far and how accurate Robbie was with his kicking. He would get the ball over the black dot on the crossbar nearly every time no matter what the angle or distance.

"I still can't believe you chose to play for your school over the regional games, what's so great about that place and that competition that would make you not want to play for your region"? Robbie asked Bootsie. No matter how hard Bootsie explained it to Robbie, he couldn't put what went on at All Kings into words to describe what a game was like there. Robbie just couldn't see it.

"Were playing against a visiting Pacific Islanders schoolboys' team this year," he told Bootsie. "You won't get that at your school."

The boys began to walk home together. "I can't wait to get back to All Kings and start the new season. I'm going to be trying to get into the senior team this year and that's going to be one tough challenge," Bootsie said to Robbie as they walked along. Soon they arrived at Robbie's house.

"Look Bootsie, I really think you should reconsider playing for the region over your school this year," Robbie said.

"Oh come on Robbie, I thought we'd agreed to disagree on this one," replied Bootsie as he gave Robbie one final wave as he walked off towards his own house, knowing full well he had some big goals to achieve this year. The following day he would be returning to All Kings to start another year and Bootsie couldn't wait.

2

The Hair

The thing that struck Bootsie the most upon his return to All Kings was that nothing seemed to have changed at all. Why he was so surprised is a mystery due to the fact that the school had been standing long before Bootsie attended there and would still be standing long after his schooldays had finished as well. If he thought his return would cause any waves in the school he was also wrong, in fact it was more like a ripple. As he unpacked his bags and set up his cubicle with some familiar items he had brought with him, he wondered if anyone even knew he had left.

Suddenly, he was tackled in his cubicle by an over-excited Razzi.
"You're back!" he said as he grappled Bootsie to the floor.
"Get off me you fool," replied a slightly unimpressed Bootsie.

"Had enough of the Charlton Hall boys have you?" asked Razzi, as both boys got to their feet.

"Yeah, something like that," replied Bootsie, "besides I wanted to come back and get you back for pushing my head into the ground last year."

"Oh, still going on about that?" asked Razzi, "It must have been someone else."

"Yeah someone else wearing the number 7 jumper," replied Bootsie as he grabbed his old friend in a headlock and began rubbing the top of his head with his knuckles.

"The hair, the hair," shouted Razzi, "don't mess up the hair!"

"Oh come on Razzi you're too ugly to worry about impressing girls anyway," said a jovial Bootsie as he released Razzi.

"Oh yeah?" said Razzi as he stood back and put up his fists in a boxing stance. "C'mon I can take ya," he added. Bootsie obliged his friend's request and shaped up in the same way. As soon as he did however, Razzi dropped his guard and said jokingly, "Nah you're a bit too big for me now, you oversized Muppet." Bootsie again grabbed his smaller friend in a headlock.

"Now I'm not going to let you go until you admit you pushed my head into the ground last year," replied Bootsie.

'OK, OK, it was me," said Razzi.

"Yeah, I knew it was you," replied Bootsie as he let a very red-faced Razzi go. Both boys looked at each other and smiled.

"It's good to have you back," said Razzi as he patted his friend on the shoulder.

"Good to be back," replied Bootsie. "Now tell me what's been going on around here since I've been away?" asked a curious Bootsie as he sat down on his bed still puffing from the struggle.

Razzi proceeded to tell Bootsie about what had happened during the time he had been at Charlton Hall. The junior boys team had had another good season but couldn't repeat their success of the previous year and had to settle for second place to a very much improved Christian Boys College team who had lost only one game for the entire season and that was against St David's who had lost most of their games and finished quite low on the table. The senior boys' team had also done reasonably well but could only manage fifth spot. Both boys were excited about moving up and trying to break into the much tougher senior boys' team and competition.

"Wait till you meet the half back we had last year. Man! Has he got a mouth on him," said Razzi to Bootsie.

"Who is it?" asked Bootsie.

"Some new boy that came here last year. He thinks he's the referee and spends most of the game telling the referee what he's doing wrong," added Razzi. "He's a pretty good player but you know what half backs can be like. What they lack in size they make up for with their mouths!" "Yeah, you're right there," replied a chuckling Bootsie, "I guess I'll meet him soon enough."

It didn't take Bootsie long to settle back into life at All Kings and feel like he had never left the place. The headmaster was especially pleased to see him return which really surprised Bootsie.

"I'm so glad to be back at All Kings again and I know I owe you a big thanks for letting me return here after spending the year at Charlton Hall," Bootsie said to the headmaster.

"And more importantly I really want to make an impression on the other boys in the senior team. I can feel good things are going to happen for us this year," added Bootsie.

"It's fine Bootsie," the headmaster said. "You're a special boy and we wouldn't dream of getting rid of you. Besides, the boy who replaced you was terrible so we are really pleased you're back and Charlton Hall can have their boy back," he added with a huge smile on his face as he looked down at Bootsie.

Bootsie was relieved to hear that he was so welcome here at All Kings. It made the transition back into the school a lot easier for him. His coach was especially pleased to see him and was keen to learn any secrets he had picked up during his time at Charlton Hall.

"How did they treat you over there?" he asked Bootsie.

"Very good," replied Bootsie.

"What about the press? Did they give you a hard time like they do here?" he also asked.

"No, not at all. Only the senior boys get written about over there for some reason, they totally leave the junior boys alone. It was great," replied Bootsie. "The senior boys get a pasting if they lose, though *our* boy journalists have got nothing on their paper," he added. His coach looked down and smiled at Bootsie.

"Some things are the same all over I guess," he said.

"Yeah I guess so," replied Bootsie with a smile.

"First training session next week, remember?" the coach said as he walked away from Bootsie.

"I'll be there. Don't worry about that," replied an eager Bootsie as he also walked away.

One thing about All Kings that Bootsie didn't know existed was the school's new weights gym. There had always been a small room with some weight-lifting equipment but since he had been away the school had sunk a lot of money into it. All the older gear had been replaced with state-of-the-art equipment and it was now all installed in a large room under the stage in the school's assembly hall. Bootsie thought it was great, it was like a dungeon under the stage and it was perfect for weight training. He knew he would be down there most days to train, as the extra weights sessions he'd done before had really given him an edge last year. Without the extra time he had spent in the Charlton Hall gym, Bootsie doubted if he could have matched it with Ox who was a naturally big rooster. It didn't really matter now, as it was all behind him and Ox was about a million miles away.

Bootsie may have thought the dungeon was great but for some reason he was in a minority and was just about the only boy who went there and used it. He had carved himself quite a muscular body with all his hard work and he knew this coming season he would have to train his heart out if he wanted to play on the senior boys' team. As he sat on one of the weight benches one day, he thought about what his first coach at the Hornets had told him about making the team and staying in the team. There was no doubt he wanted to play in the senior boys' team this year but his real dreams were much, much bigger. He also thought about what Robbie had said about playing for the region this year, but Bootsie knew that playing at All Kings would never hinder him from getting into the higher levels of the game if he stuck to what his Hornets coach had told him. Bootsie had aspired to play for his country ever since the first time he had seen a test match played. He knew that making it to the top level of the game would come from training in dungeons like this and never losing focus on his goals.

3

Where There's Smoke

The first day of pre season has always been a special day for Bootsie and today would be no different, apart from the fact that he had left wet boots in his bag, which had become quite mouldy and extremely smelly, he felt it was going to be a good day for him. He was distracted all day at school and couldn't wait to get down to the field to begin the first training run of the year. Straight after his last class he went back to his cubicle and began to get ready. He went outside and picked up his mouldy but not-so-smelly boots and took them into the bathroom to be cleaned. As he stood at the sink scrubbing off the mould, he could smell something coming from inside one of the toilet cubicles. Smoke! He turned off the tap and walked over to the door of the toilet.

"Who's in there?" he asked, to which a coughing and spluttering voice said, "Me. Now go away."

"I think I know what you're doing in there and maybe you should stop it," replied Bootsie. Just as he finished saying that the cubicle door opened and two boys walked out, filling the area around Bootsie with smoke. The boys were already coughing and the smoke started Bootsie coughing as well. As the three boys stood there coughing and spluttering the main door to the toilets opened and in walked Mr Wood.

"What are you boys doing?" he yelled as he looked at the three boys who were in the middle of a cloud of smoke. One of the boys from the cubicle spoke first, "I don't know we just walked in here."

"What!" gasped Bootsie in an astonished voice.

"All of you to the headmaster's office now," added a very angry looking Mr Wood. Bootsie and the other boys were marched into the headmaster's office to explain what Mr Wood had just come across. Bootsie sat in a stunned silence as one of the other boys told the headmaster and Mr Wood that he and his friend went into the bathroom because they thought it was on fire and they found Bootsie in there on his own with smoke coming from inside the cubicle. The other boy spoke and sheepishly backed up the first boy's story.

Finally Bootsie got to explain his side of the story to the headmaster and Mr Wood and it was the total opposite of the other boys' stories. The headmaster stood up from behind his desk.

"I'm stunned to say the least. Not only has this happened in my school but one of my scholarship selections is involved as well," he said as he looked down at the three boys. "There will be an investigation into this and until that is completed there will be no extra curricular activities for any of you and that includes rugby for you Bootsie," added a very angry headmaster. Before he could explain anymore Bootsie and the other boys were ordered to leave the headmaster's office and return to the dormitories. Once outside and away from the headmaster and Mr Wood's view, Bootsie grabbed the bigger boy by his shirtfront and held him to the wall.

"Now you listen to me you little weed, you're going to go back into the headmaster's office and tell him what's really going on here," he growled at the boy as he looked into his lying eyes.

It couldn't have been worse timing. The headmaster and Mr Wood walked around the corner and saw Bootsie holding the boy up against the wall by his shirt collar.

"Put him down," demanded Mr Wood. "Bootsie, what are you doing? This is most unlike you," added the headmaster.

"I'm trying to get him to tell you the truth," pleaded Bootsie. "I don't smoke I promise you," he told them. The two boys were ordered to leave the area by Mr Wood and they scurried off like two little rats. "We were coming to check your cubicles. I guess we'll start with yours first," said Mr Wood who was not happy.

Bootsie wasn't worried at all about the search of his cubicle. He knew he had nothing to hide, but when he opened his wardrobe door he knew he had been set up.

"My gold pocket watch!" said the headmaster in a shocked voice. "It's been missing for weeks now."

"I've never seen that before," responded Bootsie immediately. "I mean I've seen you pull it out of your pocket and look at it but I don't know how it got in there," he pleaded. The headmaster picked up his pocket watch and ordered Bootsie back to his office. Not a word was said as the three of them walked back across the grounds. Bootsie tried numerous times to defend his innocence as they walked but was stopped each time by Mr Wood.

Bootsie sat in the chair across from the headmaster's desk.
"Stealing is a non-negotiable activity in this school," stated the headmaster.
"But I don't understand. What does a non-negotiable activity mean?" replied Bootsie as he looked at the headmaster and Mr Wood with a troubled look on his face.
"Bootsie, there are six things that will

have you expelled immediately from All Kings. To the staff they are known as the six non-negotiable rules. Stealing is one of them. Surely you know how serious this matter is?" said Mr Wood.

"Yes I know from reading the rules and standards of the school booklet when I first started here. I'm not a thief, I honestly don't know where it came from," begged Bootsie.

"I fail to see how and why my gold pocket watch has ended up in your wardrobe Bootsie. This is a very serious matter and it will be treated accordingly, I am not going to make a decision on this yet," said the headmaster as he led Bootsie to his door.

Over the next few days the rumours began to spread around the school like wild fire. Bootsie's parents were called to attend the school and Bootsie had to sit there in shame as the other two boys sat in the headmaster's office and told the same story word for word. With both boys telling the same story and the fact that Mr Wood and the headmaster had seen Bootsie holding one of the boys against the wall by his shirt, it wasn't looking good for Bootsie at all. The watch being found in his wardrobe was the icing on the cake. He pleaded his case but as far as the headmaster and Mr Wood were concerned they had already made their decision. Bootsie was the first student in the history of the school to be expelled from All Kings.

"It's very sad that it has turned out like this but you have to see it from our point of view, both Mr Wood and myself found the watch in your wardrobe. Both the other boys have also told the same story about the smoking incident. They are both fine boys who have never caused any trouble like this before," said the headmaster. "I've made my decision and well I'm very sad that you have to leave on such unfortunate terms Bootsie," added the headmaster in a very quiet and gruff voice.

Bootsie was forced to do the walk of shame and return to his cubicle and collect his belongings, all under the watchful eye of Mr Wood and all the other boys who shared his dormitory. As his dad loaded the boot of his car with Bootsie's bags he turned to his son and said, "Bootsie if you tell me and Mum that what you said is the truth, then we believe you one hundred percent and we will stand by you all the way." Bootsie was so relieved that finally someone believed him.

"If we find out you've lied to us then you can imagine how crushed we will be," his dad continued.

"Honestly, I promise I am not lying about this," replied Bootsie who was on the verge of tears.

"We believe you Bootsie," his mum said as she put her arms around her son who had begun to weep.

"It's not fair! I did nothing wrong," said a very upset Bootsie over his tears.

"We know. We know, even if they can't see it," his Mum added. "C'mon let's get you home."

As Bootsie's dad drove away, Bootsie could see the two boys who had caused this to happen were standing outside one of the old unused buildings acting very suspiciously. When they looked up and noticed it was Bootsie in the back of the car they began laughing and pointing at the watches on their own wrists. He asked his dad if he would stop the car so he could confront them again.

"Let's just get out of this place," his dad said, as he continued to drive away. Bootsie slumped into the back of the seat and watched All Kings disappear away from view for the last time. By the time they arrived home it was quite late and Bootsie went straight to bed without a meal, which was very unusual for him. He loved his food. His parents knew he had done nothing wrong and seemed powerless to help their heartbroken son.

His parents allowed him to take a week off before enrolling him back into the school he had attended nearby when they first moved to the area. His first day back at the school was a nightmare; it was nothing like All Kings and Bootsie hated the place. One thing about All Kings was that most of the boys at the school went there to learn and disruptions in class were unheard of. Here, it was the total opposite and Bootsie couldn't believe the way some of the students spoke to the teachers. He tried to blend into the background but his big, muscled frame made him stand out from most of the other boys in his age group. At least Robbie was a familiar face at the school and made it a little easier for Bootsie to fit in.

Bootsie had a meeting with his new school's headmistress and she seemed very reasonable. She listened to Bootsie without interrupting him as he told her about what had really happened at All Kings. Even after ten minutes with Bootsie she could see he seemed like a very honest boy and Bootsie felt like his new headmistress wasn't doubting his word about what had *really* happened at All Kings. Although the meeting went well Bootsie still went home more depressed than ever. In his wildest dreams he didn't think he would be walking home from another school after being expelled from All Kings, especially for the reason he had been expelled for in the first place. He wanted to put it behind him and move forward but to be thought of in a way that wasn't true just ate away at him. The only way to move on was to clear his name but the only problem was he had no idea how to do it.

4

"Interesting"

When Bootsie arrived at his first Hornets training, the full impact of what had happened hit him even harder.

"Did you get your letter?" Robbie asked him as he placed his bag on the ground and began to put on his boots.

"What letter?" Bootsie replied.

"The regional camp," Robbie began to say, realising mid-sentence that his friend hadn't received a letter this year.

"No I didn't get anything," replied a very uncomfortable Bootsie.

"Oh well, maybe you'll get yours tomorrow," added Robbie, who wanted the ground to swallow him. "I'm sorry if you don't get one this year."

"It's OK, maybe it went to All Kings first," Bootsie replied knowing that the letter went to his home address last time and his mum sent it to him at All Kings. "Surely the thing at All Kings hasn't affected my chances of regional selection," Bootsie thought to himself as he began to stretch and warm up. "This is going to follow me around forever," he also thought.

Robbie introduced Bootsie to the coach and no mention was made of why there was a new boy at training. If the coach knew about Bootsie, he didn't say anything and treated him like any of the other boys. "Where do you play?" he asked Bootsie.

"I was playing at All Kings," Bootsie replied.

"No, I mean what position?" his coach said with a smile.

"Oh sorry, number 8 usually, but I can play anywhere in the forwards really," added Bootsie.

"You're a strong looking boy, I've got no doubts you're a forward," continued his coach with a smile.

"I won't be playing a single game this year at All Kings and no regional games either; the season isn't unfolding like I had planned," Bootsie thought to himself. He had put in massive amounts of time in the gym to help him move forward in his career and now he felt like it was all going to waste.

To play at the highest level, you either got selected from the regional teams or were scouted from the private schools competition into the national schoolboys' team. This year the regional schoolboys' team was playing a game against a visiting Pacific Islanders schoolboys' team as well as the usual regional games. Bootsie wasn't taking part in either of these this year and next year would be his first chance at being selected for his country at schoolboy level. His chances of selection were diminishing with every day. He was firmly back to square one and he knew it.

As he took to the field with the other Hornets players, Bootsie felt a fire burning inside him that was about to explode. He hadn't been able to get to training for the last few weeks due to what had happened at All Kings and moving back to the family home again and tonight he really felt like some contact. The Hornets had already started the season and had been smashed by the South West Storm in the first week of the competition. The team was pretty flat at training and it made Bootsie stand out even more. Robbie hadn't seen Bootsie play for a long time and he was really impressed with how good he was. None of the boys could stand up to the charging Bootsie when he had hold of the ball. It was awesome to watch Bootsie run at the defenders and then see him run over the top of them time and time again. He was like a wrecking ball at a demolition site.

"Have you ever played in the centre?" his coach asked him during a break.

"Who me? No never," replied a surprised Bootsie.

"I really think you would be a fantastic number 12 Bootsie, I can see you at inside centre no problems at all," added the coach.

"Inside centre, you mean be a back?" asked a very curious Bootsie. "But I'm a forward," he added.

"It was just a thought that's all. Mix it up a bit maybe," replied the coach.

For the rest of the night's training it was the Bootsie demolition show. He had come a long way since he had first arrived at the Hornets training a long time ago, when he couldn't even keep up and now he was a level above all the other boys in the team. Robbie was very pleased he was on Bootsie's team in the scratch match at training, as one by one Bootsie was bowling through anyone who stood in front of him. Eventually the coach had to rein Bootsie in as he didn't want any of his players getting injured before the game on Saturday.

"Do you always go this hard?" the coach asked Bootsie.

"I haven't trained for a few weeks and some things have been going on and I guess I just needed to get them out and tonight some of it came out," replied Bootsie.

"Only some of it came out tonight?" asked his coach as he smiled at Bootsie. "Do you think the rest of it can come out each Saturday for the rest of the year?"

"I guess so," replied Bootsie.

On the ride home Bootsie felt a little bit better about the situation he had been forced into, either that or it was the fact that he had just spent the evening smashing into other boys on the field and that had made him feel better about it all. Deep down he knew what was in front of him and his chances of national schoolboy selection had been seriously damaged through the actions of two weak-minded individuals who wouldn't have the guts to pull on a pair of boots each week. His parents were very understanding with him over what had happened and could easily see how it was affecting their son. Bootsie was trying to put it behind him, but each day at some point he would find himself tense up when he thought about the incident at All Kings.

Saturday soon came and it was his chance to play in a game for the first time this year. He was very keen to get to the ground and didn't wait for his parents to drive him; he jumped on his bike and was gone very early.

"This is really affecting him," his mum said to his dad on Saturday morning. "Yeah, I can see, but I don't know how we can make it any easier for him," his dad replied.

"Can you imagine how he's feeling being labelled with something that he honestly didn't do? It must be a nightmare for him going to that school everyday and listening to what the other kids must be saying about him," added his Mum.

"It's like I said, what can we do other than support him and let him know that we believe him?" replied his Dad. "C'mon let's go and watch him play, at least if he knows we're on his side it won't seem like the whole world is against him."

Bootsie's parents and sister arrived in time to see him take to the ground in the Hornet's colours again. They were pleased he had put it behind him enough to come out and play for his old team. They also knew how much he wanted his dream of playing test rugby, from day one he had told them of his dream and each week they would see him working towards it in some way and today would be no exception. When the coach threw Bootsie the number 12 jumper before the start of the game he wasn't overly surprised. He had mentioned it at training during the week and thought today would be as good a day as ever to try it out.

"If it doesn't work, I'll make some changes and put you in the forwards later in the game," his coach said. "Just do what you did at training the other night, let some more of that stuff that's building inside you come out again," he added with a smile.

What the coach didn't know was how much anger Bootsie had built up inside him, he was like a powder keg and on the field today he was ready to explode, and explode he did. From the start his tackling was ferocious; nothing or no one could get past him. Initially he hated being in the backs as he wasn't charging into as many rucks as he normally would be doing when he was a forward. What he did like and always liked was running at the opposition's defence at full pace and being the inside centre he was getting plenty of opportunities to do it. Robbie would always look for Bootsie as his first option and Bootsie would take it each time and run flat out at the defence bulldozing his way through the often weak defensive wall. It was also the first time Bootsie had played the South East Panthers as they were a new team and he made them look bad. By the end of the first half, three Panthers players were unable to take the field after being ploughed over by a rampaging Bootsie and the score was Hornets 21, Panthers 6.

"So do you want to stay at 12 or move back into the forward pack?" his coach asked Bootsie. Bootsie felt quite strange about the situation he was now in.

"I think I might stick at 12 thanks, just for today anyway," replied Bootsie. "It's pretty good doing something different," he added.

"It's fine by me, just keep doing what you're doing. Between you and me, the team has lifted to a new level since you've come and joined us," his coach said to him softly. If the rest of the team had lifted a level then in the second half Bootsie lifted two. He was on fire and continued to make the Panthers defence look weak. The Panthers were usually a good team, but today it was a one man show, the Bootsie show. Not one boy on the Panthers team was a match for Bootsie. He felt like he'd had his chances of national selection stolen from him and today he was on the road to stealing it back, so watch out anyone who was standing in his way!

By the end of the game the Hornets had easily beaten the Panthers and the final score was Hornets 42, Panthers 11. Even the Panthers' coach came over and had a word to Bootsie after the game. He was a pretty well-respected coach and had played for the region many times but never broke into the test team due to one other player at the time who was miles ahead of him in talent. That player was Bootsie's old coach at the Hornets, the 77-test veteran.

"That was some display today young man," the Panthers coach said to Bootsie, "and how come I haven't seen you at any of the regional camps?"

"I was playing in the private schoolboy competition but that fell through and last year I played overseas," replied Bootsie.

"Interesting," was all the Panthers coach said as he shook Bootsie's hand and told him again how well he had played.

"Interesting. What did that mean?" Bootsie asked his dad who was standing nearby.

"I don't know son, I don't know," he replied.

5

Connections

On the Sunday morning after the Panthers game, Bootsie wasn't sore at all, he actually felt like he hadn't even played a game the previous day. He went down to the local rugby field to do some extra fitness training; his dad had bought him some second-hand weight-lifting equipment to use at home, under the plan that every time Bootsie trained, his dad would join him. His dad had joined him once on Friday night and was still trying to recover from it, when Bootsie asked if he wanted to come down and do some more fitness training early on Sunday morning. His dad declined the offer.

Bootsie stuck to the same training pattern he had always used and today would be no different, sprints followed by sprints followed by sprints. His speed was very good for his size and he had no trouble in blitzing Robbie in a sprint race now. Actually, Robbie wouldn't even challenge Bootsie to a race any more after Bootsie had smashed him at training last week when their coach wanted to see who on the team had the goods. When tested, Bootsie delivered.

He was very pleased when his old coach walked over to him with his dog.

"I thought I'd seen a ghost," he said to Bootsie with a massive smile on his face. "Look at the size of you. My wife said she thought it was you training over here and I said it couldn't be because you go to the private school now, but when I looked outside I couldn't believe she was right. What happened, why aren't you at All Kings?" he asked Bootsie.

"It's a long story," replied Bootsie, as he tried to catch his breath.

"Well go on, tell me then," asked his old coach.

"How long have you got?" replied Bootsie trying hard to avoid the issue. "As long as it takes," the coach persisted. "Why don't you come over later and tell me about it," continued his coach.

"Sure, I'll see you a bit later on then," replied Bootsie knowing that there wasn't much point hiding it from people, after all he hadn't done anything wrong.

Bootsie went home and showered before heading over to his old coach's house. He was greeted at the door by a much, much slimmer Becky.

"Wow Bootsie, look at you," she said as she opened the door and greeted Bootsie.

"Look at me? Look at you! I would never had recognised you," he replied. "I guess they don't call you Tank any more do they?" he added, "No I haven't heard that for a while. Come in. Dad said you were coming down, he's in his study. You know where it is," she replied. Bootsie made his way down the long hall and into the coach's study, he hadn't been in here since he was given a regional camp letter and he and Robbie came down to show the coach. That day seemed like a very long time ago.

"Aagh Bootsie, I'm glad you came, I've been thinking about you since the park, now tell me what's going on and why you're not at All Kings anymore?" asked his old coach.

"Well there's no real nice way to say this, other than I got kicked out for stealing," replied Bootsie. His coach's face now resembled most people's facial expression when Bootsie told this bit of the story.

"What? You've lost me already. *You*, steal something? Surely not!" replied the coach with a shocked look on his face.

For the next twenty minutes Bootsie talked and the coach listened. He laid it all out on the table and told him everything, right from the mouldy boots he found in his bag, to putting them outside to air in the morning and then taking them into the bathroom later that afternoon to wash them, before the whole ugly smoking and watch-stealing setup had happened. His coach just nodded his head as Bootsie told him how he had been expelled from All Kings and this was probably the reason he hadn't received a regional camp selection letter this year as well. When Bootsie finished telling the story, the coach just sat there in complete silence with his hand over his mouth in deep thought.

After what seemed like forever his coach took his hand away from his mouth and said, "I'm shocked, I'm truly shocked that this has happened to you Bootsie. I hate to tell you this and you might already have realised it, but if you don't clear your name, then this will follow you around and haunt you for the rest of your rugby life. Imagine if one day in the future when you're a test player and just note that I said *when* you're a test player and not *if* you're a test player and you find yourself in a situation even remotely like this one. Straight away, the press is going to drag this up again and people will look at you very differently, no matter what the situation is." Bootsie already knew the reality that this would haunt him for a long time to come but he had never looked at it that way before, it was quite grim.

"But how can I ever clear my name now?" he asked his former coach. "Let me ring the coach at All Kings and see if I can put in a good word for you," he said to Bootsie.

"I feel terrible that I never got a chance to tell him the real truth before I had to leave. I tried but I couldn't find him to tell him," added Bootsie. "It's okay Bootsie, I know him very well," replied his coach.

"You do? How?" asked Bootsie.

"When I was finishing my career, he was just breaking into the test team. He was my second row partner for a few of his early test matches. Great player he was too. You could tell straight away he had the goods to go on with it. He never let anything get to him, the opposition, the crowds and the press, never. He is a great person and besides, he owes me more than one favour. I was the one who showed him how a lineout really works," he added. "He has kept me in touch with your development. He was pretty shattered when you went overseas last year. He rang me just after they got back from the tour and told me how big and fast you had become, looking at you today I can see what he meant. Bootsie, at least let me ring him and see if he can shed any more light on it all, okay?" he said to Bootsie who once again was stunned at what had just heard.

His coach walked Bootsie to the front door and assured him he would try his best to make something good come out of the situation he had somehow ended up in.

"In the meantime just keep training and playing for the Hornets, this mess will probably sort itself out," he said to Bootsie as they shook hands and said goodbye to one another. Bootsie could only hope his old coach was right and wished this whole thing would just go away for good. As he walked home he wondered how his life had become so complicated.

For the next two weeks Bootsie continued to train and play for the Hornets and again was a sensation for the team at inside centre *and* at his usual number 8 position. The team had racked up two good wins against the Southern Rhinos and the Eastern Raiders. This week the Hornets were up against a very tough team in the north coast Sharks, a team that had dominated the last two years of the competition. Bootsie's parents had driven the long drive to the Sharks' home ground and they had a good chat on the way up there about what was now known by the family as the 'All Kings incident'. Bootsie was in no doubt that his parents believed he had told them the truth and it was a huge worry off his mind knowing that his parents truly believed he was telling the truth. For this game, his coach put him at inside centre again hoping he could continue his good work through the middle and split the defence wide open again. As he took the field he knew that a lot of the Sharks boys had probably been selected for the regional camp and Bootsie again wanted to show anyone watching that he had been robbed of selection. The referee blew his whistle and the game was on.

From the start of the game Bootsie fired up and it continued on from where it had left off last week. He found he was a natural in his new role in the backs and loved carving up the defensive line. The Sharks were easily the best team he had faced so far since he had been back with the Hornets, but he still managed to find many gaps in their defence. Well, either found gaps or created his own by smashing his way through. It didn't really matter. What *did* matter was Bootsie had crossed the try line twice by the end of the first half and put his outside centre over, for his first try of the season as well. At half time the score was Hornets, 21, Sharks 14.

If he played well in the first half, then the second half was pretty much a copy of the first one. It was Bootsie doing what he did best, followed by support from his teammates. Most of his teammates knew why Bootsie was a wrecking ball and what had happened to him at All Kings. Whether they believed him or not, he didn't really care. He knew the truth and it was burning a hole inside him. Each time he charged at a defender or tackled one he imagined it was one of the two boys from All Kings who had told lies about him and he would smash them like he would if he could get either of them on a rugby paddock. The Sharks were very good opposition on the day and as a team were a much stronger unit than the Hornets. Bootsie was again a sensation, but his solo efforts weren't enough to win the game on his own and with Robbie away playing for the regional team, the Hornets went down by 2 points. The final score was Hornets 31, Sharks 33. It was very different to last year when the Sharks had beaten the Hornets 98 to 3 at the Hornets' home ground.

After the game Bootsie was approached by the Sharks' first-grade coach. Bootsie knew the coach had played at a pretty high level and had only recently retired from the game. The coach was stunned to hear that Bootsie had been overlooked for selection into the regional team this year and Bootsie couldn't be bothered explaining why. It made him feel good to be told about his good play by someone who really knew the game, but it wasn't helping the All Kings incident go away, or his lack of selection into the regional team.

He thanked the Sharks' coach for his kind comments and said goodbye to him.

"What did he say to you?" asked Bootsie's dad.

"Oh, you know, 'good game' and 'how come you got overlooked for the regional camp and games'. You know, the usual," replied Bootsie.

"I know it must be hard on you, but all you can do is keep trying and hope something good comes along," his dad replied.

"Yeah I know," added Bootsie. "I know."

6

The Trap

Bootsie's old coach was true to his word and he rang the coach at All Kings first thing on Monday morning. They had a lengthy discussion about Bootsie and what had happened to him with the whole incident. The All Kings coach explained to him that he had tried to express that there would have been no way that Bootsie would have been involved in the way it was made out, but the headmaster had told him his hands were tied. Even the headmaster expressed his doubts about Bootsie's involvement, but felt the school's reputation would be damaged forever if it didn't seem like strong actions were taken after the incident. He also explained that Mr Wood had walked in and found Bootsie inside the middle of a cloud of smoke and that the other two boys' stories matched word for word. Both boys had said they went into the toilets after they smelt smoke and found Bootsie in there. Both the headmaster and Mr Wood found Bootsie holding one of the boys by the shirt collar against a wall. Both boys later said that Bootsie had done it because they had told the truth about him and they were also going to tell the headmaster about the watch he had stolen. Based on that evidence, the headmaster felt he had no choice but to expel Bootsie.

The two coaches concluded their discussion about the whole ugly incident and both of them had no doubt that it was something that Bootsie simply would not do. He loved his fitness and rugby and there would be no way he would smoke and damage his health or his opportunity of fulfilling his dream. The All Kings coach said his senior team was missing a valuable player and it was a huge gap to fill. Both coaches put their heads together to try to find a way to clear Bootsie's name and possibly even get him back at All Kings.

On the Monday afternoon, the coach who usually had no time for the press, walked into the office of the school paper and closed the door behind him. The boy journalists inside were even more shocked when he turned around and locked it.

"C, c, coach how can we help you?" one of the boys stammered. "Something has happened at this school and it needs to be put right. There's a boy out there who has been labelled as a thief and you boys are going to help me put it right," he said to the group.

"Why us?" another boy asked.

"You owe it to Bootsie. You know you guys have written some pretty unfair things about him in the past few weeks. Did any of you actually investigate the other two boys, or did you just take their word for it like everyone else around here? Every week Bootsie put in more effort to a game than most people here, he loved playing for this school and I believe the truth hasn't been told yet. You boys want to be real reporters? Then start by finding out the real truth about what happened and write about it in the paper. It's called investigative journalism boys. It would make a change from stories about which player played a bad game each week that's for sure," the coach firmly said to the boy journalists.

As the coach left the office of the school paper he stood outside and listened and could hear the young journalists hotly discussing what he had just said to them.

"He's right you know," said one of the boys. "We did take the other two boys words to be the truth and didn't investigate if what they said *was* the truth. It's pretty poor on our behalf when we claim to be journalists," he added.

"Hang on a minute," firmly interjected another boy, "even our headmaster came to the same conclusion about this, and he's the one who expelled Bootsie after all. Who are we to say even *he* may have been wrong," the same boy added.

"Maybe he *was* wrong," the first boy replied. "We could at least try to find out if he did get it wrong, he doesn't need to know," he added. "OK then, let's drop the Bootsie being expelled stories for a while and let the heat die down on the issue and we'll put a few boys to work on just doing some investigation into the matter," another boy said, to which *all* the other boys agreed.

"Beautiful," the coach said to himself as he walked back to his own office pleased with what the boy journalists had decided amongst themselves.

The journalists stuck to their word and the Bootsie stories were stopped immediately. They ran a small article stating that it was time the school moved on from the issue and focused on more positive things again. The Thursday edition of the paper put the focus strictly back on rugby at All Kings and the poor performance of both teams at the start of the season. The rugby boys may have enjoyed a break from some bad press whilst the paper focused on the Bootsie issue, but true to form the heat was well and truly back on them again and the shocking start to the season *both* teams had had. The boy journalists had one boy with a camera, secretly following the two boys involved, hoping to uncover some dirt on either boy while another of the press boys began to befriend them hoping to get some information that way. The boy journalists had felt rather embarrassed that it took the school's rugby coach to point out their shortcomings and lack of research into the incident. They weren't going to let up on the matter until all avenues of enquiry had been exhausted, some of them relished the idea of playing detective instead of journalist for however long it took.

The boy journalist who began following the two boys soon uncovered a pattern about them and their routine. Every day at the same time just before dinner they would sneak off to the groundskeeper's tool shed. They would wait for him to leave and then they'd sneak inside his shed locking the door behind them. This boy relayed his information to the other boy journalists and a plan was hatched.

The groundskeeper was brought in on the plan and agreed fully to helping the boys out. He loved his rugby and had been a big fan of Bootsie in his first year at All Kings; he also knew that someone who loved rugby as much as Bootsie wouldn't be smoking cigarettes. The groundskeeper also surprisingly criticised the boy journalists for their bad press about Bootsie and not looking deeper into it before writing such rubbish about him. The boy journalists listened to what the groundskeeper had to say, then they explained to him what they needed him to do for them and he agreed with no problems. They all shook hands on the matter and the trap was set.

Like clockwork, the next day the two boys headed out to the groundskeeper's shed just before dinner. As one boy opened the door, the other boy nervously looked around to see if they had been followed. Once confident they were okay they both went inside and locked the door from the inside. Unfortunately for them, the only person who had a key to the shed had just arrived back; the groundskeeper! Both boys could hear the lock on the door being unlocked and quickly tried to make the smoke inside disappear out from a now opened window. As he opened the door he barked at the two boys, "What are you two doing in my shed?"

"We thought it was on fire," one of the boys blurted out.

"Did you? So you thought you'd lock yourself in to stop it did you?" replied the groundskeeper. The detective journalist and Mr Wood arrived on the scene as well.

"What's going on here?" he asked when he arrived and saw something wasn't right. The stronger minded boy spoke up, "We thought the shed was on fire so we came running in, and when we did, we found the groundskeeper in here smoking."

"WHAT!" screamed the groundskeeper. "Are you kidding me?"

"I've been standing behind that tree over there and watched the two of you go into the shed and then the groundskeeper came and unlocked the shed," said Mr Wood to the two now very startled boys.

"And I've been filming it," came another voice from inside the shed as a boy emerged from the smoky room. "The groundskeeper let me hide in the shed before he left today. I've just filmed the two of you smoking. Mr Wood, if you look in his pocket you'll find their cigarettes," he added. Mr Wood looked at the boy who had first spoken and told him to hand over what he had in his pocket. The boy reached into his pocket and pulled out a packet of cigarettes.

"Cigarettes, I can't believe it," said Mr Wood as he looked at the packet. "To the headmaster's office now," he ordered, "and the rest of you had better come as well and bring that camera."

Once inside the headmaster's office and faced with the mounting evidence against them, both boys gave a full confession about what had just occurred. When the weaker of the two boys started confessing he couldn't be stopped. He told the headmaster that the story about Bootsie was false and then proceeded to tell him the truth, including that the other boy was the one who had stolen the pocket watch and framed Bootsie by putting it in his wardrobe immediately after Mr Wood had told them to leave the area. It was revenge against Bootsie for pushing him up against the wall. The headmaster was shocked and must have felt extremely embarrassed that he had taken the word of what he thought were two of his best students.

He notified the two boys they would be expelled immediately and ordered them to go and pack their belongings. Their parents were called and the boys were removed from All Kings promptly and forever. They had tarnished the name of the school and what was the hardest thing to take for the headmaster was Bootsie had taken the blame for it. The headmaster thanked the journalists for their fantastic efforts in uncovering the truth and told them to run a full page, front cover, special edition of the paper immediately, letting the rest of the school know that the truth had been uncovered and Bootsie had been wrongfully blamed.

All that was left for the headmaster to do was to somehow apologise to Bootsie and try in some way to make it up to him. Not such an easy task.

7

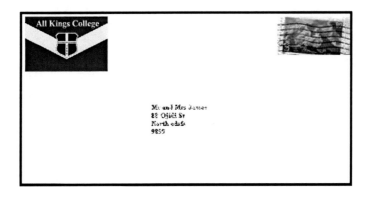

Decisions

"Bootsie, there's a phone call for you," his mum said early one morning before school.

"Who is it?" he asked.

"You'll see," she replied. Bootsie walked over to the phone and couldn't work out why his mum had such a huge smile on her face. "Hello," he said as he took the phone from her and put it to his ear. For the next five minutes the only words that came out of Bootsie's mouth were, "Oh, okay, yes, I see, uh huh, yes, and uh huh." This was the phonecall he had been waiting on for ages and when he handed the phone back to his mum he wasn't sure how he felt. The phonecall from the headmaster had now totally cleared him of any involvement in the incident but he was still very angry about it. He was pleased that the truth had come out finally but he felt really mad that the headmaster didn't believe him in the first place.

Bootsie had some serious decisions to make now and as he walked to school he was totally unsure of what to do next. He didn't like the school he was going to at the moment and the constant disruptions in class by rowdy students were very hard for him to put up with. As a school, he wanted to go back to All Kings tomorrow but the fact that he was doubted in the first place didn't sit well with him at all. He thought about his option and had to throw into the mix the fact that he had bonded with his teammates in the Hornets and they were having good success with him on the team. He didn't want to let them down by simply just up and leaving again; their coach had been great to him and never spoke about the All Kings incident once. Even the other boys in the team must have wanted to know the truth but never once asked him about it.

Two days later when Bootsie walked home from school he could see envelopes sticking out of the mail box at the family home. He pulled them out and noticed the familiar All Kings school logo on one of the envelopes. He flicked through the other envelopes which were all addressed to his parents until he got to the last one which was also addressed to him.

"This is interesting," he said as he slid his finger under the opening of the envelope and walked inside the house at the same time.

"Look at this," he said to his mum as he sat down at the kitchen table and began to read the letter out loud to her.

Dear Bootsie,

We at the regional schoolboys' rugby board have been informed about the terrible incident at All Kings School and of you later being cleared of all involvement in the matter.

We were made aware of the incident and it was the reason you were overlooked for the regional selection camp this year. As you know apart from the highest standard of playing ability it is also required that each boy selected displays a high ethical standard of behaviour off the field as well.

You have been sighted by a regional selector and we have been made aware of your outstanding efforts in the local teams competition so far this season in your games for the Northern Hornets. It is unfortunate that the regional camp has now been completed and the selections for this year's team have been made and both games against our rival regions have been completed.

We at the regional schoolboys' rugby union board would like to offer you a spot with the Regional team in the remaining game against a visiting Pacific Islanders schoolboys team that is here to play against the upcoming national schoolboys team.

We pride ourselves on our high standard of players and commend your ability to put it behind you and continue to play so well in the local competition despite the hardship you must have been facing at the time. Please contact my office on your decision as soon as possible.

President: Northern Region Rugby Union.

"I can't say I was expecting that," Bootsie said to his mum as he put down the letter.

"I thought it was a letter from All Kings," she replied.

"No that's this one," he said as he began to open the other envelope. "Let's see what they say." he added.

Dear Bootsie,

It is with the deepest of apologies that I write this letter to you today. Words cannot express how sorry I am that you were blamed for the actions of two such stupid boys. Unfortunately at the time I could only look at the evidence in front of me and due to the serious nature of the matter I had to make a harsh but what I thought at the time was the right decision.

As I told you on the phone the truth has now been fully revealed and it completely clears you of any wrong doing on your part. I can only offer you the chance to return to All Kings and continue your education here. I realise how your schooling has been interrupted already this year and do hope you return to All Kings for the remainder of your school days over this and the following year.

It seems like a small peace offering after what you have been put through but as I said it was the decision I made at the time and I believed it was the right one when I made it. I hope you have the strength of character to put this terrible incident behind you and return to All Kings.

Kind regards,
Headmaster: All Kings College.

"Now I am confused," Bootsie said as he finished reading the letter from his headmaster at All Kings. "I want to go to All Kings again but I sort of hate the place for what happened there."

"It's up to you and whatever you decide, your dad and I will support you," replied his mum.

Bootsie had quite a few decisions to make after receiving both letters on the same day. If he went back to All Kings he would have to give up playing for the Hornets and miss the regional game against the Pacific Islanders team. If he stayed, he wouldn't get the better education he would receive at All Kings or the atmosphere at each game there either. If he went back to All Kings he would be going somewhere on tour next year and who knows who was visiting the school this year. His prospects of national selection would improve if he was there as well and that wasn't a bad thing.

"I like playing with the Hornets but the competition is nowhere near as intense as it is at the private schoolboy games and each week it develops me more as a player and it's one of the things I like about the place as well," he thought to himself as he read and re-read both letters, still unsure as to what he should do. He knew someone who could help him make the decision, so he grabbed the letters and headed down the road to see him.

8

The Cap

As Bootsie sat in his former coach's study, he looked around at all the framed jumpers and photos that covered the walls. He had been a fantastic player in his day and was still considered as one of the greatest test and regional players the country had ever seen.

"Hello Bootsie," he said as he entered the room and saw Bootsie sitting on a chair in front of his desk waiting for him. "Your coach at All Kings rang me about the good news, it must feel very nice to not have that hanging around your neck anymore?" he asked as he took a seat behind his large desk.

"Yes it's nice that people know the truth about it but I can't help be angry that they didn't believe me in the first place," he replied. "Here, this is the letter from the headmaster and a surprise one I got from the regional board," added Bootsie.

The coach put on a pair of reading glasses and began to read both letters. As he did, Bootsie again looked around the room at some of the items the coach had collected over the years he had played the game.

"Hey, isn't that a St David's cap over there?" Bootsie asked his old coach as he continued to read the letters.

"What?" his coach replied as he looked up from one of the letters.

"That cap there in the frame on the wall, isn't that a St David's rugby cap?" he asked again. The coach put down the letter and looked over at where Bootsie was pointing.

"Yes it is, that is my first cap I got from St David's. I played against All Kings that day as well," replied the coach to Bootsie whose mouth was wide open.

"You mean you went to St David's?" asked a stunned Bootsie.

"Sure did," replied the coach. "Now do you want me to read these or not?"

he added as he picked up the letter again.

Bootsie sat in a stunned silence as he stared at the St David's rugby cap thinking about the coach playing for and attending St David's when he was a boy. He wondered what the games were like back then and if the crowd lined the sides of the field like they do now.

"Hmmm," said his coach as he finished reading the letters. "What are you going to do?" he asked Bootsie as he threw his reading glasses onto the desk.

"I don't know, I thought I would ask you. I had no idea you went to St David's, I didn't see the cap the last time I was here," Bootsie said.

"It was here, I've had it since I was about your age," the coach replied. "What were the games like when you were there? Were the sidelines packed with screaming and shouting spectators?" asked a very excited Bootsie.

"Yes it's exactly the same today as it was back then when I played," he replied. "I still remember some of the chants the crowd used to say," added the coach with a laugh.

"It's crazy isn't it? In my first game against Christian Boys Grammar it really got to me out there and I was terrible," said Bootsie.

"Really?" the coach laughed. "I bet the press had a field day with that," he added.

"How did you know?" replied Bootsie.

"I don't know about All Kings but I imagine it's the same. St David's had a school paper, they probably still do and during the rugby season any bad players were usually front page news," he told Bootsie.

"Yes!" Bootsie said excitedly, "It's the same at All Kings, it's called the All Kings Gazette and I've been front page news heaps of times," replied Bootsie. "I bet you were after what has just happened as well," added the coach with a grin.

Bootsie hadn't really given any thought to what the boy journalists would have written about him after he was expelled; they must have had a field day with it.

"So what about the letters, what do you think I should do?" Bootsie asked his coach.

"Bootsie, I could tell by the excitement in your voice just then, when we talked about the rugby at private schools, how much you love All Kings. If you've never seen it then you will never understand what the games are like each week," he replied to Bootsie's question.

"Yeah I know, I tried to tell Robbie what it was like but he kept saying how great the regional games were and I was missing out on it being at All Kings," said Bootsie.

"Sounds to me like you've already made your mind up then?" he asked Bootsie.

"What about the regional game and the Hornets, but?" replied Bootsie.

"Look Bootsie, you've been given an opportunity to go to All Kings when most boys can only go there if their families have a lot of money. Now I'm not saying your parents couldn't afford it, but if you hadn't been given the scholarship then I'd say you'd be going to the same school you are now. Am I right?" he asked.

"Yeah, probably," replied Bootsie.

"Going to that school and playing each week for the Hornets isn't going to give you the opportunities that All Kings will. I was lucky like you and was given a scholarship to St David's for rugby. It really set me nicely for the test team when it came time for that and I received a great education as well. I played plenty of games for the region once I left St David's so don't think your missing out on anything there," he said to Bootsie who was listening to every word he said.

"I want to go back there deep down but I don't want to let the Hornets down either and this regional game against the Pacific Islanders sounds like a nice gesture from the regional board as well," Bootsie said to his old coach.

"You don't owe the Hornets anything. They've been playing without you since you went to All Kings and yes you're a better player than most of the boys there but they can manage without you. At least go and see the boys and the coach and tell them in person of your decision to go back to All Kings, I doubt they'll hold it against you. As for the regional game, I think All Kings owes you one and I think you should put off returning there for another week and play for the regional team," he said to Bootsie.

"Yeah, I really do want to play against the Pacific Islander boys," Bootsie replied.

"Good idea, just be prepared for how hard those boys hit. Every game I ever played against a Pacific Island nation I could hardly move the next day, and don't forget to go and see the Hornets boys and coach in person, don't just leave without explaining it to them," he added.

Bootsie's former coach walked him outside again.

"Wait a second, I'll just get the dog and we'll walk back to your place with him, it's about that time of the day anyway," he said to Bootsie as he walked back inside to get the dog and his lead. As they crossed the park together the coach asked Bootsie something that he wasn't expecting.

"How is your ankle after that kick in the final match against St David's?"

"How do you know about that?" Bootsie quickly asked.

"I was there in the stands. I never miss a St David's game," he replied to Bootsie who had been frozen on the spot. "Come on, the dog wants a walk. Are you coming?" he called. As Bootsie began to walk alongside him again, the coach said, "I didn't know whether to laugh or cry when that ball went over the crossbar."

"I can't believe you were there," Bootsie replied.

"Like I said, I never miss a game, I was very pleased for you but I've got to say I was gutted for the St David's boys. My heart still lies with the black and whites. We used to hate All Kings when I was there, the two schools hated each other," added the coach.

"Nothing's changed there then," replied Bootsie as they arrived near his house.

The coach held out his massive hand and they shook hands.

"Good luck with whatever you decide but I think going back is the right decision. If you go back you'd better thank the coach there as well because he has had a lot to do with clearing your name," he told Bootsie. "Really, why?" asked Bootsie.

"Oh I think I'll let him explain that one," replied the coach as he was dragged away by his dog who was eager to continue the walk.

"All the best Bootsie," hc said as he waved goodbye and was led away by the dog.

"Yeah, same to you and thanks again," Bootsie shouted in return. "What a legend," he thought to himself as he watched his coach disappear in the distance.

Bootsie went inside and told his family of his decision to move back to All Kings.

"When do you want to go back?" his dad asked.

"Oh I think I'll let them sweat at least until Sunday without me and I'll play for the regional team this week instead," replied Bootsie.

"What about the boys at the Hornets? They are really going to miss you," added his Dad.

"Yeah, that's the only part of the plan I don't like, but a great man just told me to go and see them and explain it in person why I'm leaving," replied Bootsie.

"Sounds like the right thing to do," continued his dad. "I'll drive you there if you want, it will be quicker," he added.

"Actually I wouldn't mind riding there again it might be the last time I get to do it for a while," replied Bootsie.

Telling his teammates at the Hornets and the coach was one of the hardest things he had done in a long time. He could see on the faces of the boys that they were disappointed in him leaving. He was surprised when all of them wished him luck and hoped things went well for him when he went back at All Kings. His coach was very understanding and could see why he would want to return there as well. It turned out he was a student at St Mark's a long time ago and he knew exactly what the atmosphere at a game was like. He wished Bootsie well and hoped he would drop in at the Hornet's games or training again if he got the chance.

9

The Brick Wall

It was a great feeling to wake up early on Saturday morning knowing that he would be wearing the regional jumper again and it would be against the Pacific Islander boys. It was very rare for anyone to be given the opportunity that had been given to him; he was chosen to play for the region despite not attending the selection camp this year and that didn't happen very often. Occasionally players would be rushed into the team due to injury but most of them would have attended the camp and just not have been initially selected, but Bootsie hadn't been to the camp for the last two years. He was treated fairly by the other boys in the team as they waited by the buses that would be taking them to the stadium for the friendly match.

Bootsie had been given a regional tracksuit during the week and on the morning of the game there were plenty of boys getting ready to board the buses, so other than Robbie, not many people knew Bootsie hadn't been to the camp. Bootsie sat next to Robbie on the bus and on the way to the stadium he explained the *whole* story to him. Robbie was astounded by what Bootsie told him and he kept quiet for pretty much the entire trip to the ground. He still couldn't understand why Bootsie wanted to play private schoolboys rugby at All Kings and not play for the Hornets.

"If that's what you want then go for it," he said to Bootsie. Bootsie was going to go for it, but today he wanted nothing more than to get another opportunity to play for his region again.

The boys were directed to the change rooms to get ready for the game. "Good luck and I'll see you after the game," said Robbie as they were getting off the bus outside the stadium.

"What?" asked Bootsie, looking confused.

"I'm not playing today," replied Robbie.

"What do you mean your *not* playing?" Bootsie asked.

"Look Bootsie, I didn't want to say anything incase it made you more nervous about today but you're easily the youngest player in your whole team today. You're going to be playing against some much older and bigger boys in this game. I simply didn't get selected to play today, I just get to sit back and watch the action unfold," Robbie replied.

"Just how much bigger are these boys then?" asked a slightly worried-looking Bootsie.

"Guess you'll find out soon enough," replied Robbie with a huge smirk on his face as he walked away to find his seat in the grandstand.

As he sat in the change rooms Bootsie looked around at some of the other boys in the team and felt like he was the only one in his age group in there. None of the other boys noticed that he was younger than most of them, probably due to his size and strong build. Most of them thought he'd been at the camp and was brought in due to injury. The next person to walk into the change rooms was also a shock to him.

Bootsie was unaware that the North Coast Sharks first-grade coach was also one of the regional selectors. He noticed Bootsie sitting on the bench looking slightly nervous and walked over and wished him well. "I heard all about the incident at All Kings," he said to Bootsie as he approached him. "I'm so pleased it's all worked out in the end and you still get the opportunity to play for the region today. I'm just glad I got to see you play in that game against the Sharks earlier in the season. You really impressed me with your performance that day. I couldn't stop thinking about how good you were and why you weren't playing for the regional side. I did some digging around and found out why you couldn't be selected for the regional games. Once I was told the truth had been revealed I demanded you get to play for us today," the coach added. I only wish you had got to play in your age-group games. We might have had some more luck with you tearing through the centre and beaten those Southern boys," he said to Bootsie with a smile.

"The centres?" Bootsie said rather nervously.

"Yeah," replied the coach. "You are a centre aren't you?" he asked Bootsie.

"Um no, normally I play number 8. It

was just a trial thing for a few weeks at the Hornets," replied Bootsie with a bit of a grin.

"Well, from what I saw against our boys, you make a great centre and today you'll be wearing 12," he said to Bootsie as he patted him on the shoulder and wished him well.

When Bootsie got changed and was handed his jumper it certainly had number 12 on the back, he even checked it again and had another look just to be sure before he put it on.

'Older boys... out of position... might have bitten off more than I can chew here," he thought to himself. He remembered something coach Van Den had said to the Bulldogs once, "Do you know what to do when you've bitten off more than you can chew?" he asked the boys. "Start chewing!" he replied. The saying stuck with

Bootsie ever since and today he would be chewing. He ran into the stadium with the rest of his teammates and was surprised at how many people were already at the ground for the game. There was still another game between a combined armed forces team and a Pacific Islanders 'A' team after this game which was the curtain raiser to the main game tonight. He looked around at some of his teammates and saw some of them looked like lambs to the slaughter; the noise of the crowd was already getting to them and the game hadn't even started yet. Fortunately for Bootsie, large crowds were no longer a problem for him, but he was looking at a much bigger problem, his opposite number was huge and was glaring at Bootsie. The referee blew his whistle and it was action stations.

The Northern Region team was receiving the ball and after it was caught, it was offloaded to Bootsie from the first pass. He tried to step off but was met by a sea of red, white and blue jumpers who crunched him to the ground. Bootsie had the sense to hang onto the ball and make it available at the back of the ruck that had formed over him. The half back was soon at the back of the ruck and the ball was out again, Bootsie picked himself up from the ruck and began chasing the play. He had to constantly stop himself from flying into the rucks and let the team's forwards do that. He had only played a few games at inside centre and the change from number 8 was a lot harder at this level. After the opening twenty minutes he settled into the role a bit easier and soon found himself in position to receive the ball from the fly half and do his thing.

Bootsie had a very strong build for his age but when he ran into the Pacific Islanders defensive line it was like running into a brick wall. Each time he did it, he felt like the crash test dummy used for testing cars before they went to market. Each impact was just like a car crash. By half time Bootsie was glad for the break. The Pacific Islander boys had a handy lead and at half time the score was Pacific Islanders 21, Northern Region 3.

The Northern Region's coach was very good at half time and only asked the boys to give one hundred percent for the rest of the game. He knew the Pacific Islander boys were here to play the national schoolboys team the following week and they were expected to be very competitive against them. Bootsie was already hurting and had never played against such strong opposition before. The combined boys' team was made up of players from three of the Pacific Nations and they were an awesome and hard-hitting bunch of boys. Bootsie picked himself up from the bench in the changing rooms and wondered how he was going to make it through the next 40 minutes.

The second half started the same way the first half had; big hits, big tackles and lots of impact. The Northern Region forwards were having a really tough time with a much bigger Pacific Islanders forward pack. They were getting smashed at the scrum and each time it was set, the Pacific Islander boys just pushed the scrum back until it collapsed, putting heaps of pressure on the Northern Region's half back. When they did get quick ball Bootsie found he was only able to run half the distance he usually did, before either running into a brick wall or being brought to ground in a tackle. Each time he would go to ground he could feel how hard the Pacific Islander boys were hitting in the rucks. No wonder the forwards were suffering, if some of the noises coming from the impacts were anything to go by.

This game was a game that a lot of men wouldn't want to play in; some of the opposition boys were like giants and that was taking its toll on the injury bench. All the forwards had been replaced and some of the front row had to come on again due to more injuries. It would have been easier to go with uncontested scrums but the Northern Region coach didn't want to lose all sense of pride, so the least injured of the front row players were put back out there. Bootsie was patched up a few times for cuts and grazes. He joked to a teammate after the game that it was lucky that he had used his face to take most of the impact. By the end of the game the Pacific Islander boys looked like they had been in a training game and the Northern Region boys looked like they were returning from a war. The final score was Pacific Islands 63, Northern Region 10.

The Northern Region boys made a guard of honour for the combined armed forces team to run through before their game and by the looks on some of their faces as they ran out past the beaten bunch in front of them, it wouldn't have boosted their confidence at all. The Pacific Islanders first grade team would be playing against the Northern Region's first grade team later tonight after the main game and Bootsie couldn't wait. Bootsie watched the main game sitting next to Robbie and already he was hurting, he couldn't begin to imagine how bad it would be in the morning.

10

The All Kin

Thursday Edition

BOOTSIE IS INNOCENT

After a startling investigation into the earlier incident involving drugs at All Kings and the eventual expulsion of our scholarship boy Bootsie it has now been revealed that all was not right and the wrong boy had been expelled from the school. Late on Friday afternoon an undercover operation caught the real offenders red handed and with surveillance used there was no way these two boys would be framing

another poor innocent boy. Stay tuned to the Gazette for further updates on this breaking story. Our beloved Head Master has also informed the paper that a letter will been sent to Bootsies home in an attempt to get him to come back to All Kings. Hopefully we can get him back and we can all be blessed with not only a wonderful rugby player for the school but a wonderful student in general.

Ren
foll
imp

The
that
rela
the
beh
of a
expr
in li
its
beh
con
or v

The Apology

For some reason the words of his former coach made more sense to Bootsie as he tried to get out of bed the following morning. "Be prepared for how hard those boys hit. Every game I played against the Pacific Islanders I could hardly move the next day." How true those words were now. Bootsie lay back down in his bed and every inch of movement was horrific. At some point he was going to have to get up and make his way back to All Kings before dinner as was the rule for anyone taking weekend leave. He stayed in bed for as long as he could before being tempted by a hot bath that was run for him. He eased his aching body into the hot water and decided he would never get out again. Eventually his toes and fingers resembled old prunes and even *he* thought it was time to get out.

For the rest of the day he moved around the house like an old man, groaning each time he had to move more than an arm's length.

"Are we doing a weight session today?" his dad joked at the breakfast-cum-lunch table.

"Good one Dad," was Bootsie's response.

"Don't forget you've still got to pack yet and you haven't got much time before we have to leave," his mum said.

"I know. I just didn't think I would be hurting this much, those boys were like brick walls," he said to his slightly sympathetic parents. "Great game to watch," his dad said to him, "and you've got another jumper to put in with the others," he added. Bootsie had swapped his number 12 jumper with the Pacific Islanders number 12 player, except his new jumper was a few sizes bigger than the one he had been wearing last night. As he tried to eat he couldn't imagine how the front row boys must have been feeling today.

After lunch Bootsie's mum helped him pack his bags for the trip down to All Kings. She had sent the school a letter stating that Bootsie would be returning today and would arrive on time before the main meal, which was served at 6 p.m. She had also telephoned the school just in case and spoken to a very pleased headmaster who was very happy that Bootsie had made the decision to return to the school on Sunday. He did try to talk them into returning earlier so Bootsie could play for the school on Saturday but she told him that Bootsie wanted to play for the regional team this week and she believed that he and the school owed Bootsie this request. He told her he fully understood and looked forward to seeing him on Monday morning when he could deliver his apology to Bootsie in person.

Bootsie slept for pretty much the entire trip down to All Kings, the previous night's game had really taken it out of him, not to mention the emotional roller coaster he had been riding for the last few months. Both he and his parents hoped that the rest of the year would be a lot more stable for him and they could put the start of the year behind them forever.

Bootsie awoke from his sleep just as his mum drove up the entrance road to the familiar grounds at All Kings. He grabbed his bags from the back of the car and said goodbye to his mum who stayed by the car. His dad helped him carry the bags to his dormitory. As he walked in there was a huge banner stretched from one side of the large building to the other. It said

"WELCOME BACK BOOTSIE" in big black bold letters. It was so different from the ripple he created when he first came back at the start of the year; this was more like a wave. He said goodbye to his dad who wished him well as he gave his son a huge hug, but Bootsie quickly let him know he was still very sore and a light one would have done.

He should have told Razzi the same thing because he came barrelling into Bootsie's cubicle and grabbed his old friend in a huge bear hug nearly crushing Bootsie's already aching body.

"Razzi, Razzi," Bootsie gasped, "Please let go of me," he added in a weak and totally exhausted voice.

"What happened to you?" Razzi asked him as he stood back to look at a very bruised Bootsie.

"I played in the regional game yesterday evening against the Pacific Islander boys, it was a tough game to say the least," he replied to Razzi who was smiling from ear to ear.

"I heard the regional first grade team got smashed; I guess by the look of you that your team had a similar result?" Razzi asked.

"Yeah we got hammered and today I'm feeling every minute of it," replied Bootsie as he lifted his suitcase on the bed and began to unpack. "Pretty tough in the forwards was it?" Razzi asked.

"Yeah it was, but I played in the backs," he replied.

"In the what?" asked a stunned Razzi who was shaking his head as he sat on Bootsie's bed.

"You should have seen the size of their forwards, they were monsters," added Bootsie as he continued to tell Razzi about the game.

Bootsie soon unpacked and before long it was time to make his way to the dining hall for dinner. As he hobbled his weary and tired body to the dining hall he was shown a copy of the last edition of the school paper. The front cover read, "BOOTSIE IS INNOCENT" in bold letters. He took a copy of the paper and not long after dinner he lay on his bed and read the front page story.

After a startling investigation into the earlier incident involving theft at All Kings and the eventual expulsion of our scholarship boy 'Bootsie' it has now been revealed that all was not right and the wrong boy had been ex-pelled from the school. Late on Friday afternoon an undercover operation caught the real offenders red-handed and with the surveillance used, there was no way these two boys would be framing another poor innocent boy. Stay tuned to the Gazette for further updates on this breaking story. Our beloved headmaster has also informed the paper that a letter will been sent to Bootsie's home in an attempt to get him to come back to All Kings. Hopefully we can get him back and we can all be blessed with not only a wonderful rugby player for the school but a wonderful student in general.

As he read the paper, he was joined in his cubicle by some of the boy journalists. They were very honest and told Bootsie that they had written some terrible things about him when the story first came out. They felt they had learnt some valuable lessons that could help them in their future careers in journalism. One by one they shook Bootsie's hand, apologised and told him they were glad he was back and the real truth had been revealed. Bootsie was slightly lost for words and accepted their apologies even though he hadn't read any of what they had written about him. He could imagine from the way they wrote about boys who didn't play well each week, that with something juicy like what had happened, they would be brutal. One of them also told him that if the coach hadn't come and seen them that they probably would never had seen the error in judgement they had made.

Bootsie couldn't wait to see his coach again to thank him for what he had done as he was pretty much responsible for the truth being revealed. Bootsie eventually tracked him down the next morning and couldn't get the words of thank you out quickly enough.

"I'm just glad the truth came out in the end," his coach said.

"Yeah, it was pretty hard to be accused of it and then expelled for something I didn't and would never do," replied Bootsie.

"The truth *always* comes out at some point son," added his coach. "Besides I'm more intrigued as to why you were playing number 12 on Saturday," he said to Bootsie with a huge smile on his face.

"Oh yeah, *that*. I meant to talk to you about that," said Bootsie with a sheepish look on his face.

"Its fine Bootsie, I'm just glad to see you back here," added his coach as he patted him on his shoulder.

Bootsie had one more person to see before he could really let go of this ugly incident for the last time. So, straight after he said goodbye to the coach he headed for the headmaster's office without an invitation. Bootsie told the headmaster's secretary that he was expected. When he was led into the office, the headmaster seemed quite startled to see him.

"I honestly don't know how to say sorry to you Bootsie," he said as he stood up from behind his desk to shake Bootsie's hand. "I was wrong and I apologise," he added. Bootsie could see in his headmaster's eyes that he was truly sorry for what had happened and the simple words, *I'm sorry* from the humbled headmaster were enough for Bootsie. He remembered that his dad had once told him that it takes a real man to admit when he is sorry. Bootsie thought of this now and he fully accepted the headmaster's apology and it was *never* mentioned between the two of them again.

"You're the first person that I can tell. I've just been on the phone and organised a game between All Kings and the visiting Pacific Islanders schoolboys this Thursday before they play the national schoolboys' side," said the headmaster, looking very pleased with himself. Bootsie suddenly felt weak, as though all the blood had drained out of his body.

"Are you okay son? You've gone very pale," he said to Bootsie.

"I'm fine," he squeaked back, not quite believing what he had just heard the headmaster say to him.

"That's good. I'm glad you're okay because I was going to make a decision on the tour for next year sometime today and seeing you're here, you can help me with it right now." With that, and a huge smile on his face, the headmaster reached into his top pocket and pulled out a familiar looking red leather case and handed Bootsie a dart. He called in his secretary and handed her the third dart and shut the door behind her. They all stood next to each other in a line in front of the map. Then the headmaster spoke, "Ready for the tour next year? One.., two.., three.., *throw!*"

The End.

Check out the Bootsie website
www.bootsiebooks.com

Thanks to KooGa Rugby
www.kooga.com.au

Lightning Source UK Ltd.
Milton Keynes UK
UKOW04f1945060116

265945UK00001B/16/P